SPIDERS SET II

WHITE-TAILED SPIDERS

Jill C. Wheeler
ABDO Publishing Company

New Hanover County Public Library
201 Chestnut Street
Wilmington, NC 28401

visit us at
www.abdopub.com

Published by ABDO Publishing Company, 4940 Viking Drive, Edina, Minnesota 55435. Copyright © 2006 by Abdo Consulting Group, Inc. International copyrights reserved in all countries. No part of this book may be reproduced in any form without written permission from the publisher. The Checkerboard Library™ is a trademark and logo of ABDO Publishing Company.

Printed in the United States.

Cover Photo: David McClenaghan / CSIRO
Interior Photos: Animals Animals p. 19; AP/Wide World pp. 5, 21; CSIRO pp. 11, 15, 18; Dr. J White p. 7; Peter Arnold p. 6; The Queensland Museum pp. 13, 17; University of Southern Queensland p. 9

Series Coordinator: Stephanie Hedlund
Editors: Stephanie Hedlund, Megan Murphy
Art Direction: Neil Klinepier

Special thanks to Mr. Ron Atkinson of the University of Southern Queensland for his help with this project.

Library of Congress Cataloging-in-Publication Data

Wheeler, Jill C., 1964-
    White-tailed spiders / Jill C. Wheeler.
      p. cm. -- (Spiders. Set II)
    Includes bibliographical references.
    ISBN 1-59679-297-3
    1. White-tailed spiders--Juvenile literature. I. Title.

QL458.42.L3W49 2006
595.4'4--dc22

2005045215

Contents

WHITE-TAILED SPIDERS 4

SIZES 6

SHAPES 8

COLORS 10

WHERE THEY LIVE 12

SENSES 14

DEFENSE 16

FOOD 18

BABIES 20

GLOSSARY 22

WEB SITES 23

INDEX 24

White-Tailed Spiders

All spiders are **arachnids**. Scorpions, ticks, and mites are, too. Arachnids have two body parts and eight legs. All arachnids are also **arthropods**. That means their skeletons are on the outside of their bodies.

There are more than 100 spider **families** in the world. White-tailed spiders belong to the Lamponidae family. There are about 60 species in this family. They only live in Australia and New Zealand.

Many people do not like white-tailed spiders. They believe bites from these spiders cause major skin problems. However, scientists have found no proof of this. Most bites simply lead to itching and swelling around the bite.

But, many people still fear white-tailed spiders. Some people kill them whenever they see them, which is unfortunate. The white-tailed spider is a skilled hunter that helps keep populations of other spiders low.

In addition to white-tailed spiders, many other kinds of spiders are found in Australia and New Zealand. So, these countries are popular among arachnologists, or people who study spiders.

SIZES

The world's largest spider is the goliath tarantula. It is found in South America. It has a leg span of 11 inches (28 cm). The world's smallest spider is an orb web spider from the South Pacific island of Samoa. Its body is about the size of a pinhead.

A young goliath tarantula

White-tailed spiders molt, or shed their outer skeleton, as they grow.

White-tailed spiders are larger than a pinhead, but they are still small spiders. An adult white-tailed spider fits easily on a half-dollar coin. Its long, spindly legs are each about as wide as a pin.

Like many other spiders, white-tailed females are larger than males. Females grow to be about 20/32 of an inch (16 mm) long. Males may grow to about 15/32 of an inch (12 mm) long.

SHAPES

White-tailed spiders are easy to identify. Their bodies are long and tapered. They have eight eyes and eight long, thin legs. They also have two **chelicerae** and two **pedipalps**.

Like all spiders, white-tailed spiders have two body parts. The head and **thorax** make up the front body part. It is also called the **cephalothorax**. The wide, rear body part is called the abdomen. Male white-tailed spiders have a hard, narrow plate at the front of their abdomen.

All white-tailed spiders have special tufts of hairs on the ends of their legs. These hairs let the spiders walk on smooth or sloping surfaces.

White-tailed spiders can spin silk using their **spinnerets**. Sometimes they spin temporary resting places made of silk. Yet they do not live in webs. This makes them a little different from many other spiders.

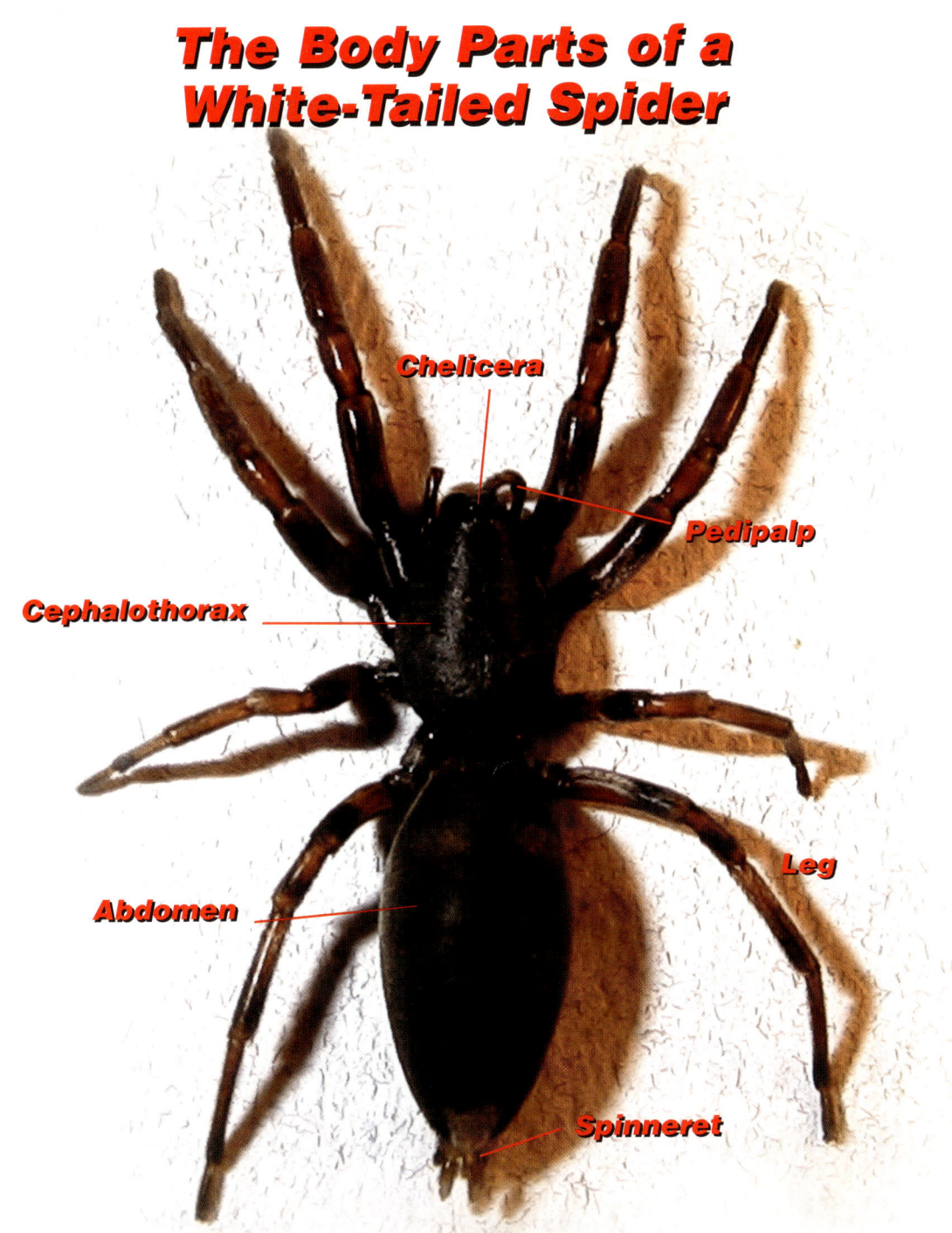

Colors

White-tailed spiders got their name from the white or gray spots at the tip of the abdomen. Young spiders may also have four or more pale spots on the upper abdomen. These spots become harder to see as the spider ages.

The body of the white-tailed spider is dark red to gray. Their glossy legs are dark with orange brown bands on them. Their coloring helps them blend into their **habitat**.

Not all spiders are dull colors. Some, such as crab spiders, are bright so they can hide on flowers. Other brightly colored spiders let enemies know they are poisonous.

The spots on the top of the abdomen fade as a white-tailed spider ages. These spots are also harder to see right after the spider molts.

WHERE THEY LIVE

The most common species of white-tailed spiders are the *Lampona cylindrata* and the *Lampona murina*. These spiders are found in Australia and New Zealand.

White-tailed spiders live in **urban** areas, forests, and woodlands. They like to live in cool, dark places. They seek shelter under tree bark and rocks. They may also live under fallen leaves or piles of logs.

In urban areas, white-tailed spiders make their homes in gardens and sheds. Sometimes they get inside houses. There, they hide in out-of-the-way corners. They also hide in bedding and in clothes left on the floor!

White-tailed spiders do not build or live in webs like many other spiders. They are hunters that move from place to place to find food. They are most active in the summer and early fall.

Opposite page: *When in Australia and New Zealand, make sure to shake out clothes that were lying on the floor. This will help you avoid a white-tailed spider bite.*

Senses

Most spiders have eight eyes. Some only have six, and cave-dwelling spiders may not have any eyes. White-tailed spiders have eight eyes that are grouped close together. But like most spiders, they do not see very well at all.

Because they hunt at night, white-tailed spiders have large eyes. These eyes let in a lot of light, so the spiders can see shapes in the dark. But during the day, their large eyes let in too much light. So, they often sneak into houses to avoid the bright light of day.

Because of their poor eyesight, white-tailed spiders must rely on other senses to survive. The bodies and legs of all spiders are covered in fine hairs. They use these hairs to sense vibrations and air currents. This lets them sense when a meal or **predator** is nearby.

All animals create vibrations when they move. Spiders use the hairs on their bodies and legs to follow the movements of the creatures around them.

DEFENSE

Like most spiders, white-tailed spiders must be wary of birds and large insects. Small animals sometimes eat spiders, too. Humans and even house cats can also be enemies.

The white-tailed spider's first defense is to hide. They hide under branches, leaves, and other debris during the day. They only hunt and move around at night.

The second defense of white-tailed spiders is to bite and then run away. These spiders do not go after people or pets. However, they will bite if they are afraid. If they are cornered, they can bite again and again.

White-tailed spiders are usually slow moving. But, they can move quickly in short bursts. That is normal for hunting spiders. It helps them get away from their enemies. It also helps them catch their prey.

White-tailed spiders can run quickly in short bursts. They may use this speed to get away from predators and find a hiding spot.

Food

White-tailed spiders like to eat other spiders. Their favorite foods include black house spiders and daddy longlegs spiders.

Most white-tailed spiders wander into houses in search of black house spiders. Some Australians and New Zealanders may brag about never seeing spiders in their homes. This could be because they have a white-tailed spider living with them!

White-tailed spiders are skilled hunters. First, they approach the web of another spider. Then, they pluck at the outside strings of the spider's web with their legs.

A black house spider is a white-tailed spider's favorite meal.

The white-tailed spider does this to make it seem like an insect has become trapped in the web. Soon, the other spider rushes out. It thinks it is going to find a meal. However, it may soon become the white-tailed spider's dinner!

After the spider is caught, the white-tailed spider bites the victim with its fangs. These fangs are located on the **chelicerae**. Spiders eat their prey by **injecting** it with **digestive** juices. The juices turn the prey's insides to mush. Then, the spider sucks out the mush.

Some spiders eat larger prey than the white-tailed spider. However, every spider digests its food outside its body and then eats it.

Babies

White-tailed spiders spin pink, disk-shaped egg sacs out of silk. Each sac can contain up to 90 eggs. Female spiders always attach their egg sacs to something. Outside, they attach them under bark or stones.

Female white-tailed spiders guard their egg sacs carefully. They watch over them for about three weeks, and then the eggs hatch. Cold weather can delay the eggs from hatching. That is why spiders often put their egg sacs in or near houses. They stay warmer that way.

Baby spiders are called spiderlings. After hatching, the white-tailed spiderlings leave their mother and go out on their own. They are able to start hunting small prey right away.

Opposite page: *White-tailed spiderlings are ready to hunt as soon as they hatch. Other spiderlings cannot hunt right away. Instead, the mother carries her young until they are ready, such as this wolf spider.*

Glossary

arachnid (uh-RAK-nuhd) - an order of animals with two body parts and eight legs.

arthropod - a member of the phylum Arthropoda with an exterior skeleton.

cephalothorax (seh-fuh-luh-THAWR-aks) - the front body part of an arachnid that has the head and thorax.

chelicera (kih-LIH-suh-ruh) - either of the leglike organs of a spider that has a fang attached to it.

digestive - of or relating to the breakdown of food into substances small enough for the body to absorb.

family - a group that scientists use to classify similar plants or animals. It ranks above a genus and below an order.

habitat - a place where a living thing is naturally found.

inject - to forcefully introduce a fluid into the body, usually with a needle or something sharp.

pedipalp (PEH-duh-palp) - either of the leglike organs of a spider that are used to sense motion and catch prey.

predator - an animal that kills and eats other animals.

spinneret - either of the two body parts attached to the abdomen of a spider where the silk is made.

thorax - part of the front body of an arachnid that contains the head and lungs.

urban - of or relating to a city.

WEB SITES

To learn more about white-tailed spiders, visit ABDO Publishing Company on the World Wide Web at **www.abdopub.com**. Web sites about these spiders are featured on our Book Links page. These links are routinely monitored and updated to provide the most current information available.

INDEX

A

abdomen 8, 10
arthropods 4
Australia 4, 12, 18

B

bites 4, 16

C

cephalothorax 8
chelicerae 8, 19
color 10
crab spider 10

D

defense 10, 14, 16

E

egg sac 20
eyes 8, 14

F

families 4
fangs 19

food 12, 14, 16, 18, 19, 20

G

goliath tarantula 6

H

homes 12
hunting 5, 12, 14, 16, 18, 19, 20

L

Lamponidae 4
legs 4, 7, 8, 10, 14, 18

M

mites 4

N

New Zealand 4, 12, 18

O

orb web spider 6

P

pedipalps 8
predators 5, 14, 16

S

Samoa 6
scorpions 4
senses 14
silk 8, 20
size 7, 8
skeletons 4
South America 6
species 4, 6, 10, 12, 14, 16, 18
speed 16
spiderlings 20
spinnerets 8

T

ticks 4

V

vibrations 14

W

webs 8, 12, 18, 19

ML 11/05